FULL METAL
TRENCH COAT

Dean A. Anderson

To my kids, Bret, Paige and Jill – Bill's first clients.

And to Savannah Kynoch, whose father, Josh, fought the good fight.

BILL THE WARTHOG MYSTERIES: FULL METAL TRENCH COAT
©2011 by Dean Anderson, seventh printing
ISBN 10: 1-58411-068-6
ISBN 13: 978-1-58411-068-2
Legacy reorder# LP48301
JUVENILE FICTION / Religious / Christian

Legacy Press
P.O. Box 261129
San Diego, CA 92196
www.LegacyPressKids.com

MIX
Paper from
responsible sources
FSC® C048831

Cover and Interior Illustrator: Dave Carleson

Scriptures are from the *Holy Bible: New International Version* (North American Edition), ©1973, 1978, 1984 by the International Bible Society. Used by permission of Zondervan Bible Publishers.

Printed in the United States of America

Table Of Contents

Chapter 1

The Case of the Full Metal Trench Coat

I don't suppose you have a friend who is a warthog. You probably don't have a friend who is a professional detective, either. So it's very unlikely that you have a friend who's both.

But I do.

Oh, wait a minute. Before I tell you about my friend, I should tell you who I am. My name's Nick Sayga, but a lot of kids call me "Ten Toes" because I sometimes play video games with my feet. That used to be the strangest thing about me.

Then I became friends with Bill the Warthog, Private Detective.

When you have a detective for a friend, you get

asked to help solve cases. Sometimes people bring cases to Bill. Other times, he sees a case that needs him before anyone else even notices.

I guess I'd better give you an example of what I mean.

One day, Bill was over at my house. Our back yard really needed mowing, so I told Bill he could chew on the lawn. (Bill enjoys munching on the grass – if he finds bugs in it he considers them a bonus!)

Bill came to my house dressed the way he usually is when he's out in public: dress shoes on his hind feet, dress pants, white shirt, tie, long trench coat. Oh, and he always wears a fedora hat (like the ones men wore in those old black-and-white movies).

I was helping Bill out of his coat so he could start snacking on the lawn, but we were interrupted.

Tommy Hendricks came by on his bike and told us he was gathering all his friends together to meet his cousin Brewster. According to Tommy, Brewster had a great business opportunity he wanted to tell us about.

"Get all your money together and come over to my house," Tommy called as he rode off.

This certainly got my attention (it's hard to make good money when you're 12), so I told Bill I thought we should go. But as I said, detectives look at things differently. (I think warthogs look at things differently, too.)

"Sounds like a case," Bill said.

"But Tommy called it a 'business opportunity,'" I said.

Bill sighed as he looked down at the grass and realized he'd have to skip his snack. "Well, we'll find out which it is soon enough."

I went in to my room and found ten bucks to stick in my pocket, along with some change.

When we got to Tommy's house, there were about fifteen kids hanging out in the garage. Tommy was introducing Brewster to everyone.

Brewster looked to be four or five years older than the rest of us (except Bill). The way he acted kind of reminded me of guys I'd seen on TV commercials who were selling used cars.

Tommy brought him over to Bill and me. "This is Nick Sayga and his friend, Bill. Bill is a…"

"Detective," Bill interrupted.

"Cool," Brewster said as he looked closely at Bill's

tusks and hairy face. "If this company gets big, maybe you can be our mascot."

Bill did not seem thrilled with the idea.

"All right, everyone take your seats," Brewster said.

There were about ten lawn chairs surrounding what looked like a couple of cardboard refrigerator boxes taped together. Bill and I, and a couple of other kids, stood in the back.

"I know this box doesn't look like much," Brewster began, "because it isn't much. But inside this box is an incredible machine that could make all of us a fortune.

"But before I tell you about my machine, let me tell you what led to the idea for it. Do any of you have bronzed baby shoes at home?"

I didn't know what he was talking about, but about five kids raised their hands.

"Growing up, I was always fascinated by these shoes on a plaque that my mother kept on her dresser," Brewster said as he held up a piece of wood with two brown baby shoes glued on it. "My mother took my baby shoes to a man who covered them with bronze so she could keep my first shoes safe forever.

"One day, I looked at those bronzed shoes, and it

gave me an idea. I thought how cool it would be if we could have metal clothes. If they were flexible, you would be much safer wearing them.

"I thought how safe we could be on skateboards and bikes if we had metal covered clothes. I first started working on bronze, but then I tried silver and even gold.

"And so I have perfected my machine. I just need your financial backing to apply for a patent for this machine. And if you give me money, you'll get a percentage of the profits. The more you give, the more you'll get.

"But I don't expect you to invest without a demonstration. Could someone donate an article of clothing?"

No one moved. "How about that trench coat, sir?" Brewster said as he looked right at Bill. "I would think it would be good for a detective to have a full metal trench coat to protect you from bullets and stuff."

"My jobs don't get me in those kinds of situations," Bill said. "But I'll let you experiment with my coat anyway."

I knew the reason Bill took the risk was because he had five or six coats just like that one in his office.

Brewster put the brown coat in the box. The machine made loud whirring noises, and we could hear clanging metal.

Then Brewster came out with Bill's trench coat. It was no longer brown, but gold.

Brewster threw the coat to me, and it felt the same, but it was indeed covered with gold. I flung it to Bill, who caught it on his tusks. He tossed it high in the air, sliding his front legs through the arm holes as it came down.

"I feel you are perpetrating a fraud here," Bill said as he glared at Tommy. "And I don't take this lightly. This obviously isn't gold. You're trying to cheat these kids out of their money!

"Besides, we don't need this kind of armor; we only need the Ephesians armor that Paul wrote about."

How did Bill know so quickly that the trench coat wasn't real gold? And what is the other armor Bill was talking about?

☞ Turn to page 90 to find out!

Chapter 2

The Case of the Warthog of War

"I'm thinking about making copies of this comic and selling them at school," my friend Mike Reed said after ball practice one day.

He handed me the stapled pages. "I'd like to sell ads, too, and make some money. But would you please ask Bill to read it first and tell me what he thinks?"

"Why do you want Bill to read it?" I asked as I folded up the paper and crammed it in my pocket.

"Oh, you'll see," said Mike.

Mike had been making comics for years. But up until now his superheroes always had been human beings.

I pulled the comic back out of my pocket to look it over. When I saw the title – "Phil the Warthog: Warthog of War" – I knew why Mike wanted Bill to see it.

I laughed and told Mike that there are few people out there who would believe a warthog could be a detective, let alone a super soldier. But Mike said believability wasn't a high priority in the world of comics.

After a quick stop at home for lunch, I rode my bike over to Bill's office.

"So what is this, Nick?" Bill asked as I handed him the folded papers.

"Mike Reed drew a comic with a new character. Since there was a bit of resemblance to you, he thought you might want to look it over."

"Sure, let's look at it together."

The cover showed a warthog wearing an American G.I. helmet and a green uniform. He was holding a bazooka aimed at the reader.

"Does Mike know that warthogs in the wild work very hard to avoid fights?" Bill asked.

I shrugged my shoulders as I read on.

The beginning of the comic told how Phil the Warthog came to be.

It opened in the laboratory of a mad scientist, Dr. Werner von Doomcough. He was in the midst of experimenting on a warthog, giving it the power of speech and super strength.

Bill stopped reading and turned to me. "Why is there always a mad scientist in these stories?"

"Because you can't have something as outrageous as a talking warthog in a story without some kind of explanation for how it learned to talk, can you?" I regretted the words as soon as they were out of my mouth.

There was an uncomfortable silence.

"I mean," I said, "you can't have a creature with super strength without explaining that, can you?"

"Well, I see your point there."

We kept reading. The next part of the story had Shady Tompkins, a United States Special Forces officer, breaking into the mad scientist's lab and freeing all the lab animals. But he took the warthog back to the U.S. government's secret labs.

Bill stopped reading again. "Have you ever told my story to Mike?"

"Well, I might have mentioned a thing or two about your past."

"Did you mention that I was rescued from that horrible Pottersville Zoo by Shannon Thompson? Did

you mention that she brought me home to be raised with her family? Shady Tompkins is a pretty similar name."

"I might have mentioned a detail or two."

We read on. In the comic, they named the warthog "Phil" and trained him in the ways of war. He was fed only worms and grubs, and he always slept outside.

Phil was constantly engaged in war games on the "Danger Patio." The government workers didn't give him anything to read except books and magazines about weapons and battle strategy.

I could tell Bill was getting into the comic now. "That poor warthog!" Bill said, shaking his head. "Couldn't they have given him something decent to read? I would have been lost without my Sherlock Holmes and Father Brown – and Encyclopedia Brown for that matter!"

And then in the comic…oh, I'll just copy the dialogue right from it:

Shady: So, Phil, did you finish reading that text on

the Hundred Years War?

Phil: Yeah, but I'm not sure how accurate it was. Especially when it quoted that general saying, "So we begin the Hundred Years War."

Shady: I suppose that was unlikely.

Phil: But Shady, why have I only learned about warfare? Why haven't I been taught more about science, literature, history or choreography?

("Good point!" Bill interjected.)

Shady: We have taught you all you need to know to be a good soldier.

Phil: But why do I need to be a good soldier?

Shady: Because there is a battle coming, Phil, a big battle.

Then we had to turn some pages past ads Mike was hoping to sell to the local comic book store and ice cream parlor. Then it was back to Phil and Shady.

Phil: Who are we going to battle, Shady?

Shady: I'm afraid to tell you.

Phil: No, it can't be.

Shady: Yes, it can be.

Phil: Don't tell me.

Shady: I have to tell you, Phil.

Phil: Is it?

Shady: Yes, we're going to battle Dr. Werner von Doomcough.

("I saw that coming," Bill said.)

Phil: But that's not all we're facing, is it?

Shady: No, it's not, Phil. Dr. Doomcough has built an army of invisible soldiers, and we must stop them before they get to Hog Town. We must prepare for battle.

Phil: All right, but before we go to battle the invisible soldiers, I want to know the weather report. Will it be sunny or rainy?

And then came those dreaded words:

To Be Continued...

"So, what did you think?" I asked Bill.

"I'll wait and tell Mike."

We went to the Reeds' house, and Mike rushed out to meet us out front. "So, what did you think?" he asked.

"First of all, let me say the artwork was very good," Bill said. "I'm not sure anyone can capture the full majesty of the warthog on the page, but the backgrounds and human beings were very lifelike."

"Thank you," said Mike. "But what I really wanted to know was what you thought of Phil. Do you mind?"

"Do I mind that you based a few details about your character on me?" Bill asked. "Not at all. Artists need to borrow from real life all the time.

"But I do wonder whether war is the best subject for your kid readers to be thinking about. And there were some things that were just too hard to believe."

"You mean like the invisible soldiers?" Mike asked.

"I mean like a warthog only eating worms and grubs. We need our veggies and roughage. I have no problem with invisible enemies – you can find out about them if you read in the right places."

"But would you read the next Phil comic?" Mike asked.

"I suppose, but I already know what kind of weather Phil was looking for when he said 'sunny or rainy.'"

"Yes, I suppose you do," said Mike.

What kind of weather would Phil have been looking for? And was Bill serious when he said there are real invisible enemies?

☞ Turn to page 92 to find out!

Chapter 3

The Case of the Milk and Money Belt

Sometimes people can take pride in the weirdest things. I know, because I do.

I'm proud of the fact that I have a higher score on the video game "Mounties of Montreal" than any other kid at my school (and that's with them using their hands and me using my feet!).

My friends have proud moments, too. Blake "The Tongue" Lewis never misses a chance to show off his ability to touch his tongue to the bridge of his nose.

And Bobby Clover takes pride in two things: his expert ability at milk tasting, and the money belt he won at the county fair for milk tasting. Bobby could guess with one taste which dairy the milk was from,

and often the cow's breed. So he won the fair prize, which was a belt made from intertwined dollar bills with fifty-cent pieces glued on it. It was kind of ugly, but money is money.

So when Bobby told me he had bet his money belt on a milk-tasting contest with Chris Franklin, I thought something odd was going on. Chris was a school bully who was always looking for trouble.

During recess, I asked Bobby how it came about.

"At lunch I was sitting at a table," Bobby explained, "when Chris came up with his gang. He started bragging about how he could taste milk better than I could. I said, 'There's no way.'

"Then one of his buddies took a swig of milk from a carton and sprayed it in my face and said, 'What kind of milk was that, expert?' I got really mad and was going to go tell the lunchroom monitor, but Chris stood in my way.

"He said, 'Hey, no reason to make a big deal out of this. How about if you prove to me that you are an expert? I'll bet your money belt against twenty bucks that I can beat you in a milk-tasting contest.'"

"So you took the bet?" I asked.

"Yeah, Nick. I knew I could win a tasting contest

with Chris, no sweat," Bobby said.

"Hey, Bobby, did you ever think that maybe Chris just wanted you to bring out your money belt so he could steal it?"

"Um, no. But that does make sense."

"When and where is the contest? I could come with a friend of mine to make sure everything is on the up and up."

I called Bill after school and asked him to meet Bobby and me at the Elm Street Park the next day at 4 p.m.

Bill met Bobby and me at the swing set. Bobby was carrying his money belt. Then the three of us walked over to Chris and his pals, Dwayne and Josh, who were at the picnic tables.

There was a cooler by a tree, and there were paper cups and two blindfolds on one of the tables.

"What are the blindfolds for?" Bill asked.

"I just thought they would make things more interesting," Chris said. "I don't even need to taste the milk; I can smell it and tell whether it's whole, non-fat, or whatever."

"No way," Bobby said. "No one could tell that by smell."

"Maybe you can't, but I can," Chris said. "Willing to bet your belt on it?"

"Sure," said Bobby.

"He's up to something," Bill said to Bobby.

"Aw, close your tusks, Bill," Chris said. "He already agreed."

Chris said the way the contest would work was Chris and Bobby would be blindfolded. Dwayne would pour a type of milk in a cup, then hold it a foot away from Bobby, and then Chris, and they would guess. Whoever guessed the best of five would be the winner.

I was thinking maybe Chris and Dwayne had figured out the order of the milks ahead of time, so I insisted that I be the one to choose which milk to use.

I chose the whole milk first. I held the milk near Bobby.

"Can you guess, Bobby?" I asked.

"I don't know, Nick," Bobby said. "No one could know."

Dwayne held the cup near Chris and said, "You'll

totally guess this one, Chris."

"Is it whole milk?" Chris asked.

I was amazed. Chris had guessed right.

Next, I got the nonfat milk. "Can you guess this one, Bobby?"

"I don't know – is it the whole milk again?" Bobby asked in a small voice.

"Nothing can stop you now, Chris," said Dwayne as he held the milk in front of Chris.

"It's the non-fat," Chris said.

If Chris could guess the next one, he would win the best of five. Of the milks we hadn't used in the cooler, there was still chocolate milk, soy and two-percent. I went with the two-percent.

"Okay, Bobby," I said. "You need to get this one."

"I'll guess whole milk again," he said.

"All right, Chris, I know you'll get this right, too," Dwayne said.

"Um, give me a second. It's...um...two-percent."

"That's right," I said. "I guess Chris wins."

Chris and Bobby took off their blindfolds.

"You didn't even get one right," Chris said to Bobby. "Very lame. So hand over the belt."

"Not so fast," said Bill. "I think another contest will

be needed. One that is honest this time."

"What do you mean?" Chris said. "Nick was watching the whole thing. This was an honest contest."

"Let's have a talk in private."

Bill and Chris went off, then came back.

Chris said, "All right, we'll do another contest. But this time we'll be tasting the milk, not smelling. And it won't be for money."

This time, Josh and Bill poured the milk. Bobby guessed all five, while Chris could only guess the chocolate milk.

"Okay, you win," said Chris. "But as we said, no one has to pay up."

"And we know who the honest winner is," Bill said. "Bobby, you can keep your money belt. And Chris, I think you should consider getting a new belt, the belt of truth."

How did Chris cheat in the first contest? And what is this "belt of truth" Bill was talking about?

☞ Turn to page 94 to find out!

Chapter 4

The Case of the Celebrity Shoes

I think Joel came up with the idea of tennis balls on the tusks so Bill could join the team.

All the guys wanted Bill to be able to join the neighborhood soccer league, because he was good. Real good.

First, he was fast (warthogs can run thirty miles an hour).

Second, he had a nose for the ball. (Bill said he loved the smell of plastic in the morning – it smelled "like victory.")

And third, he could never be called for "hands."

The problem was that he kept puncturing soccer

balls with his tusks, and we were afraid he might accidentally gore somebody. But with the tennis balls covering the pointy ends of his tusks, he was able to play.

I thought I would never see anything as odd as a warthog wearing a trench coat and fedora hat. But that was before I saw a warthog in soccer shorts and a T-shirt. And it was before I saw the Lemon Street Team in uniform.

There are six teams in our neighborhood league. All the teams are named after a street. Bill and I play for Maple Street, then there's Lemon, Poplar, Fig, Fir and Apple Street Teams.

During the summer, we all got together to have fund-raisers for team uniforms. We divided the money evenly between the teams, and each team was able to spend the money on the uniforms they chose.

Our first game was on a Saturday afternoon at the Maple Street Elementary School playground. We were in our new silver and black uniforms (which were pretty cool even if my mom did help pick them out), waiting for the Lemon Street Team.

Then the Lemon Streeters came. They weren't wearing matching uniforms – they had an assortment of T-shirts and shorts that you could tell had been pulled blindly out of drawers just before they came. But they all had very large shoes.

We all shook hands, and I talked to Blake Lewis, a friend of mine on the Lemons. "Hey, Blake, didn't you guys get your share of the money for the uniforms?"

"Yeah, we did, Nick. Get a load of these," Blake said, holding his right foot high.

"Okay, it's a shoe. Why didn't you get new uniforms?"

"This isn't just a shoe – this is a professional shoe."

"What do you mean?"

"Well, Cameron Smith, that guy over there, managed to get us professional soccer shoes. You ever heard of Manchester United?"

"Yeah," I said. It's probably the most famous British soccer team. "Didn't Beckham play for them?"

"I think so. Anyway, they only use shoes for one game. They get new shoes for every game.

"Cameron's uncle is an equipment manager for Manchester United, and he was able to get hold of a dozen pairs of shoes. The shoes didn't even cost anything; we just had to pay for the shipping."

"And I'm guessing the cost of shipping was the

same amount as the money you had for uniforms?" asked Bill, who apparently had been listening in.

"Yeah," Blake said slowly as he sized up Bill, then turned back to me. "Hey, that thing talks! I thought he was your mascot!"

"He doesn't just talk," I said. "He also plays a mean game of soccer. Speaking of which, we should start playing."

With Bill's help we whupped Lemon Street hard that day. Final score: 7-1. I don't think it helped that at least half of the Lemon Streeters were wearing shoes that were too large for their feet. But after the game I wasn't proud of my team.

Joel and some of the other guys started to tease Blake, Cameron and the others about the uniforms. "You look like bums!" – that kind of thing.

"You're just jealous of our Manchester United shoes!" Blake said.

Then Joel asked, "Were they really worn by professionals?"

"They certainly were," Cameron replied. "And if you're interested, I could get professional shoes for you."

"They didn't make you play like pros," Joel said.

"But you think it would be cool to have pro shoes," Cameron said, and Joel nodded in agreement.

"I could get more shoes," said Cameron. "Of course, my uncle cut me a deal for just the shipping cost since it was for my team. But for the right price, I could set up you and anyone else who's interested in a pair."

"I'm not much of a tennis shoe wearer," said Bill, "But I would be interested in proof that these shoes have been worn by English pros."

"Why don't you show him the letter?" said Blake.

"What letter?" asked Bill.

"I have a letter from my uncle authenticating the shoes," said Cameron. "You guys can come to my house to see it."

I knew chores awaited me at home, and the same may have been true for others, because everyone on both teams suddenly seemed interested in seeing the letter.

Once we arrived at Cameron's house, he had us wait in the back yard while he went to get the letter for Bill to inspect. Here's what it said:

Dear Cameron,

Here are the tennis shoes I promised to send you. This letter is to verify that these shoes have all been worn for one game by the Manchester United professional soccer team.

I hope your team wears them proudly.

Sincerely,
Your Uncle Henry
Equipment Manager
Manchester United

"I'd think that's all the proof you need," said Cameron.

"I'm afraid it is," said Bill. "Proof that you cheated your team out of its uniform money. I'm guessing you spent a bit on shoes at the thrift store and kept the rest of the money for yourself."

"Is that true?" Blake asked.

"It's true," Bill said. "But I just don't understand this human fixation on footwear.

"If you're going to worry about such things, concentrate on Paul's Good News shoes in Ephesians. Those are the only ones that really matter."

Why did Bill think Cameron was dishonest? And what are the Good News shoes?

☞ Turn to page 96 to find out!

Chapter 5

The Case of the Flying Rocks

It was a beautiful, warm Saturday afternoon, and I should have been outside playing, according to my mom. But then I might have missed Bill's latest client.

By an amazing coincidence, I was playing the video game "Handyman Harry" when Brandon Cutter knocked on my door.

(If you've played "Handyman Harry," you know what I mean when I say I was in the Hardware Store of Doom section, collecting my toolbox pieces. I had my hammers, ball-peen and claw; my screwdrivers, Phillips and straight edge; and my drill; but I still needed to get my saws, screws and nails.)

It was a coincidence because Brandon wants to be a handyman. He's been trying to start a handyman business the last couple of years, but not many adults hire sixth-graders to rebuild their cabinets or install chandeliers.

Still, he has built a fairly steady business of mowing lawns. He was knocking on my door because his business was in danger.

"I think it was Chris Franklin, Nick," Brandon said.

"That's often the answer, but what was the question?" I asked. Chris was the neighborhood bully.

"Someone's been sabotaging my gardening business, and I was wondering if your detective friend could help me."

Brandon waited until Bill came over before telling his whole story.

"I've been building my customer base the last couple of years. I mow most of the lawns in the neighborhood. But last week, someone put these flyers on car windows."

The flyer said:

> Brandon Cutter Grasses Cutting Business
> I Cut Grass Real Good for Only $100 a Lawn.

"The flyers weren't only on the car windows. They

were all over the lawns, too. And $100 is much more than I charge.

"Anyway, Chris Franklin went around picking the flyers off the lawns and knocking on the doors asking if he could mow lawns for a dollar less than I usually charge. I lost two customers.

"But something worse happened. I went to mow the Smiths' lawn. They're my best customers, and they always tip well. But when I was mowing next to their giant living room windows, my lawn mower shield fell off."

"What is the lawn mower shield?" I asked.

"It's a solid plastic piece that keeps grass from flying all over. And it helps keep rocks and sticks from flying up."

"Is that ever a problem?"

"It was today," Brandon said, "There were a bunch of rocks in the Smiths' lawn by their living room windows. The rocks cracked the windows."

"Are you suggesting your lawn mower was sabotaged?" Bill asked. "Couldn't the shield have fallen off on its own?"

"I check my lawn mower after every job. Clean off the blades, tighten all the screws. I don't see how it

could have come off. Not only did Mr. Smith fire me, he says I have to pay $500 to repair the windows."

"Where do you keep your lawn mower?" Bill asked.

"In my tool shed."

"Did you notice anything out of place in the tool shed?" Bill continued.

"I don't remember," Brandon said.

"Let's go," Bill said.

In Brandon's tool shed, his work desk was scattered with tools.

"Were these tools lying out when you left, Brandon?" Bill asked.

"I put them away last night. But this afternoon I just came in and got the lawn mower and left. They might have been out. I don't know."

"Well, we can at least find out if Chris is responsible," said Bill. "Or not. Brandon, do you have any refreshing beverages?"

"We have lemonade," said Brandon.

"Perfect," said Bill. "Pour four glasses. And Nick, get Chris Franklin."

It took a bit to persuade Chris to come to Brandon's tool shed. But eventually I asked if he wasn't coming because he was scared of Bill, and then he came out of pride.

Brandon's tool shed was well stocked. (He had every tool "Handyman Harry" could get – and more.)

"First of all," Bill said when Chris and I got there, "let's have some lemonade."

As I said, it was a warm day, so lemonade sounded good to all of us. There was a full pitcher,

along with four full glasses. We all drank up, and Brandon carefully took the glasses back to the kitchen.

"I understand you've developed an interest in lawn mowing," Bill said to Chris.

"That doesn't mean I have anything to do with the flyers or the Smiths' windows," Chris said.

"Good. We can cut to the point," said Bill. "I think someone sabotaged Brandon's mower. I think someone loosened the screws on the lawn mower shield and put rocks on the lawn next to the Smiths' windows."

"How do you know Brandon isn't just doing sloppy work? But even if someone sabotaged the mower, you couldn't prove it was me," Chris taunted.

"I keep my mower in perfect running order," Brandon protested, coming out of the kitchen.

"I was thinking of dusting for fingerprints on some of Brandon's tools," said Bill.

"What good would that do you, if you don't have fingerprints to compare 'em to?" asked Chris.

"Oh, I have some fingerprint samples on the lemonade glasses that Brandon just took back to the kitchen. So I'll know if Nick was the one who sabotaged the lawn mower."

I was pretty sure Bill was joking.

Chris glared at Bill, then walked over to the worktable, picked up a screwdriver and dropped it into the lemonade pitcher.

"Oops!" Chris said.

"Brandon, did you see that?" Bill asked.

"I saw that," Brandon said.

"Nick, did you see that?" Bill asked.

"Yeah, I guess," I said. I really wasn't sure what I was supposed to see, but I didn't want to disappoint Bill, who obviously was pleased with himself.

"Did you see that, Mr. Smith?" Bill asked.

Mr. Smith walked into the tool shed. "I did, Mr.

Warthog. I was watching through that knothole in the tool shed wall."

"What did you see?" Chris asked.

"We all saw enough to know you sabotaged the lawn mower shield," Bill said. "And I see that you need to get a shield for yourself, Chris. The shield of faith, not a lawn mower shield."

What did Bill see that proved Chris's guilt? And what is the "shield of faith"?

☞ Turn to page 98 to find out!

48

Chapter 6

The Case of the Edible Arrows

I was sure Bill was going to cancel out on going to the movies.

He usually hates movies, especially detective movies. ("All gunfights and car chases," he complains. "I've never even been in a pie fight or a bike chase, not that I'd want to.")

But this was a documentary about Africa, *Savannah Sunrise*, and it was playing in 3-D on the new Humongo screen in town. Bill was hoping he might see some of his family in the crowd shots.

Still, when a case came up, Bill usually dropped everything. And a case did come up.

Charlie Palm came into Bill's office while I was visiting, enjoying a lazy spring break afternoon. We had helped Charlie before with his cookie business. Now he had a new problem.

Charlie had decided the trend was health food, and he wanted to make something that would help kids enjoy carrots and celery. So he designed the Arrow Press.

The Arrow Press was a kitchen device that would cut a piece of carrot or celery or even broccoli into the shape of an arrow. You could use the celery and the celery strings to make a bow for your veggie arrows. Then you could shoot the veggie arrows into dip.

The presses had been selling well, so I wondered what the problem was.

"I'll tell you what the problem is," said Charlie. "Someone says an edible carrot put his eye out."

"Wow," I said in disbelief, "you always hear mothers warning about that, but you never think…" I didn't finish the sentence.

"Well, his eye isn't really out, but he says it's hurt," said Charlie.

"Who is the alleged victim? And what does he say happened?" Bill asked.

"Matt Manford says his three-year-old sister, Michelle, got hold of a celery bow and shot a carrot into Matt's eye. Now Matt's blind in one eye and he's going to have to wear an eye patch."

"I hear the pirate look is in," I added, rather unhelpfully.

"Manford...I know that name," said Bill. "Aren't they the ones who just won the lawsuit against that fast-food restaurant, claiming there was a mouse in their milk shake?"

"I think so," said Charlie.

"They've made thousands in lawsuits, usually settled out of court," said Bill.

"Matt offered to settle the case out of court if I paid him my three months' profits."

"How much would that come to?" I asked.

"About a thousand dollars, Nick," said Charlie.

"That's a lot of money," I said.

"But not as much as I might have to pay if this goes to court," said Charlie. "My dad says the lawyer fees alone could be over a thousand. So settling out of court is sounding good."

"But something sounds fishy about this," said Bill. "As have a lot of the Manford lawsuits. Rumor has it they bought their own mouse from the pet store for that milk shake, but the restaurant just didn't want to bother with a lawsuit."

"There is something fishy about this," said Charlie. "There is no way the celery string would have enough force to actually hurt someone. I'm sure Matt's just counting on my paying to end the whole thing."

"I'm taking the case," said Bill.

After Charlie left, I said to Bill, "I suppose this means we're not going to the movies."

"Not at all," said Bill, "I'm more eager to go than ever. But I'm afraid I have to take care of some errands before the show. I'll meet you at the theater."

My parents dropped me off at the theater. There was a pretty big crowd there for the show, but I noticed someone in particular: Matt Manford, with his family. He was wearing the eye patch on his right eye.

The movie was pretty cool. The 3-D made it look like the elephant was charging out of the screen right at you. I could have done without the lions eating the zebra in 3-D, though.

But there were warthogs, so Bill was happy.

I still was baffled as to why he was willing to take a break in the middle of a case to go to the movies.

As Bill and I were walking out of the theater, I saw a booth with a sign that read: "Take a quick survey for a free movie pass!"

Anything free is good when you're 12 and have to live on a $5 a week allowance, so I asked Bill if we should take the survey. He said, "I'm not paying for any more movie passes than I have to."

I started to ask Bill what he meant, but then my parents came to pick me up, and I forgot about it.

The next day, Bill called and asked me to bring a pen and notebook, and to meet him at the Manfords' house. We rang the bell and a small girl (I'd guess it was Matt's little sister) answered the door. Bill asked her to get Matt.

Matt came to the door and asked why we were there. He had his eye patch on, but it looked a bit skewed. Like he had just put it on – quickly.

"I'm here to ask you a few more questions about the movie survey you took last night," said Bill.

"Hey, aren't you that warthog detective?" Matt asked.

"Yes, I am," said Bill. "But investigating and poll-taking are not that different. Both jobs are just a matter of gathering information."

"So what do I get if I answer more questions?"

"More free movie passes," Bill said.

"Sounds good to me," said Matt. "I may never pay for a movie again. I got passes for taking the survey last night, and now this!"

"In answering the survey," Bill began, "you said, 'It seemed like the lion was leaping out of the screen and into the audience.' How would you phrase that for a movie poster?"

"I might be quoted in a movie poster? Okay, how's this: 'I was sure the lion was leaping right at me'?"

"Great," said Bill. "Here are your movie passes, and here is an agreement to drop your suit against Charlie Palm. Matt, you really should worry less about edible arrows and more about the enemy's arrows that tempt you to lie."

How could Bill prove Matt was lying? And what are the enemy arrows he is talking about?

☞ Turn to page 100 to find out!

Chapter 7

The Case of the Hopeless Helmet

A fact about warthogs that you're not likely to find in *National Geographic* is that they are hopeless skateboarders. Maybe I'm over- generalizing. But I can say with certainty that Bill cannot skate.

My church sets up a skateboard park in the back parking lot on weekdays during the summer. They put out some decent bowls and ramps, so it's a cool place to hang out.

The way it works is they have a set time for open skate, and then one of the youth group leaders gives a talk about Jesus. (Some kids leave when the talk starts, but most figure the quality of the ramps

outweighs any potential for boredom.)

I wanted to invite Bill to it. But I thought he might like to give skateboarding a shot on the flat driveway at our house first.

He definitely could not balance on his hind feet on one board – that didn't work at all. So we tried two skateboards, one under the hind feet and the other under the front feet – that didn't work so well either. So he said he'd just watch us at the skate park instead.

They had put up a new grind bar, so I was having fun with that when I saw Mark Canard take a spill on the big ramp. The leaders – and a lot of kids curious to see if there was blood – surrounded him right away.

The guy in charge, Tim Eagle, asked Mark how many fingers he was holding up. And who was president. And what was Spiderman's secret identity. Then he said Mark was okay. He told Mark to consider himself fortunate and that he ought to get a better helmet.

Bill and I went over to talk to Mark, and I could see what Tim meant about the helmet. Mark was holding two halves of a "safety" helmet in his hands. It looked to be made of foam.

"Hey, Mark, are you okay?" I asked.

"Yeah, Nick. Some knee and elbow cuts and scrapes, and a cut on my forehead. Otherwise, I'm okay."

"It's good your knees and elbows hit the pavement before your noggin," said Bill. "It could have been a lot worse."

"Yeah," said Mark. "Tim said I should get a new helmet. I don't understand how this came apart. The guy who sold it to me said this helmet was top of the line."

"Which store did you buy it from?" Bill asked.

"Oh, it wasn't a store. I got it from Zack, a guy in the neighborhood. He says stores just rip you off."

"How much did he charge you for this, Mark?" I asked as I took half of the helmet from his hands. It didn't take much pressure to break the half into quarters.

"It was only five dollars," said Mark. "That's a lot less than they charge in the stores."

"I suppose so," said Bill. "Can you tell us where we can find this Zack fellow?"

We went to Oak Street, where finding Zack was not a problem.

We saw an older kid (fifteen or sixteen years old)

practicing his skateboard Ollies on the sidewalk. He was wearing shorts, a long-sleeve shirt, knee and elbow pads and a helmet.

"Are you Zack?" Bill asked.

"Yeah, what are you?" he responded.

"Just another prospective customer," Bill said.

"No," said Zack. "What are you?"

"Oh, I'm also a private investigator," said Bill. "But enough of that. Would you be willing to sell me one of your fine helmets?"

"If you've got the money," said Zack, wiping the sweat from his forehead with his sleeve. "Wait here a minute."

Zack went in the front door of his house, and then we saw the garage door open. The garage was full of cardboard boxes, but toward the front was a spinning rack, covered with helmets.

"I've got a lot of helmets, but I'm not sure I've got any that would fit a…whatever you are," said Zack.

"Oh, it's not for me. It's for my friend Nick here," Bill said, nodding toward me.

"Yeah, I'm sure I have his size, or close enough."

"Are all of those helmets made of foam?" I asked.

"Oh, it's not foam," Zack said. "These are all made

with the latest technological substance called 'Absorbacon.'"

"I don't know. It doesn't look too safe to me," I said.

"What do you know?" asked Zack. "You're a young punk. I've been skating for years and I know what's safe." Zack lifted his right hand and put it through his helmet chin strap to scratch the stubble on his neck (I think to emphasize the fact that he was older than me).

"How much are you charging for these helmets?" Bill asked.

"Five bucks apiece," said Zack. "It's quite the deal."

"It's not a deal if it endangers the health and safety of young skateboarders," Bill said.

"What are you talking about?" said Zack. "I know as much about skateboard safety as anyone. I've skated for years."

"Just observing you today, Zack, has convinced me you don't know enough about skateboard safety. And it is important to have a secure helmet. Not as important as the helmet of salvation, but important."

"What are you saying?" said Zack.

"I'm saying we're going to have to put you out of business."

How did Bill observe that Zack didn't know about skateboard safety? And what is this "helmet of salvation" he was talking about?

☞ Turn to page 102 to find out!

Chapter 8

The Case of the Pizza Sword

As I believe I've mentioned more than once, I got the nickname "Ten Toes" from playing video games with my feet. I've even steered the wheel of the Dizzy Dizzy Driver game with my foot. Of course, in public places I have to keep my shoes on, which is more of a challenge, but it's doable.

But that technique won't work for the great new game at Merlin's Pizza Parlor. It's called "Dragon Destiny," and you get to handle a real sword.

Well, it's a realistic-looking rubber sword. It has some kind of motion sensor technology so you can

use the sword to fight a nasty-looking dragon on the screen.

Anyway, it's a great game, and I wanted to show it to Bill, so I asked him to meet me at Merlin's. We went inside, but the game's sword was missing.

"Now I've got you, you thieving kid!"

The voice came from behind us, and I turned to see Marty, the owner of Merlin's, grabbing Bill by the shoulders.

Bill broke Marty's grip and turned around.

"Oh, I'm so sorry," Marty spluttered. "You're not him. I don't know what you are, but you're not him. Who is this um, fellow, Nick?"

"Marty, this is my friend," I said. "His name's Bill. He's a warthog and a detective. Who did you think he was?"

"I thought he was the kid on the security tape," Marty said. "The kid who stole my sword."

Marty took us to his office to show us the tape. "This tape is from three days ago," Marty said. "The camera only shows the counter area, but see that kid in the trench coat there? When he came in, the game had a sword. When he left, the sword was gone."

"I know that guy," I said. "That's Trevor Black. He

goes to my school."

"The tape doesn't actually show the theft," Bill said. "But he could certainly hide a four-foot sword under a trench coat."

"Hey, didn't you say you're a detective? Could you look into this?" Marty asked.

"Perhaps," said Bill. "If the price is right."

Bill didn't worry about his pay so much when he took kids' cases. But when it was a case for adults, he could be a tough negotiator.

They finally settled on a fee of three months of free pizzas with toppings that Bill would bring in himself, such as insects and lawn clippings. (Bill often said, "Nothing sets off the taste of mozzarella like crickets and Bermuda blue grass.")

Bill looked up Trevor's address in the phone book. The Blacks' house was within walking distance of Merlin's, so we headed right over.

We found a rather surprising sign posted on the Blacks' front lawn. It read:

World's Best Arthurian Museum!
See authentic relics of King Arthur
and his knights in garage.
$1 admittance fee.

Trevor was on a stool by a card table at the side door of his garage.

"Hey, Nick!" he called out. "Come to see the museum?"

"Maybe," I said. "How's business?"

"Not bad. I've already made about 50 dollars. Hey, isn't that your friend, the one I've heard about? You're from Africa, aren't you?"

"Originally, yes," said Bill.

"I have a theory that the knight, Sir Lancelot, was exiled to Africa."

"Interesting," said Bill as he pulled two dollars from his wallet. "I'd like to hear more."

We went into the garage. There were a variety of displays, in glass cases and mounted on the walls.

"King Arthur lived in the 500s AD," said Trevor, "in England with his knights. People continue to be fascinated by the reign of this great king and his quest to spread justice in the ancient world."

"It still hasn't been established whether King

Arthur was real or a legend, has it?" asked Bill.

"Well, I think all the authentic items in this museum clearly demonstrate that King Arthur was real," Trevor replied.

Bill and I wandered around the garage museum. All of the items had little descriptive plaques telling what they were.

A plaque next to a handkerchief said Lady Guinevere had used the handkerchief on the day she wed King Arthur. A shield was said to have belonged to Sir Percival and used on his quest for the Holy Grail. And there was some kind of old-fashioned guitar that had belonged to Sir Robin.

A large, flat case had a big Bible in it. The Bible was opened to a printed "Family Tree" page signed by King Arthur and all the Knights of the Round Table. The plaque by the Bible explained that Arthur had all the knights sign that page because he thought of them as his brothers.

As I turned from the Bible, I let out a small gasp when I saw what Bill was looking at on the wall. It was a sword! I was sure it had been taken from the video game at Merlin's.

"I suppose that's King Arthur's sword?" I asked.

"No, Excalibur has never been found," said Trevor. "But I believe this sword belonged to Lancelot."

"You wouldn't mind if we took down that sword to examine its authenticity?" I asked.

"I certainly would mind," Trevor said. "All the items in this museum are extremely valuable, and I won't let anyone handle them."

"No need," said Bill. "We have enough evidence that this museum is a fraud. Trevor, you need to refund everyone's money and return the sword to Merlin's."

"But you barely looked at it," Trevor protested.

"My evidence comes from a different sword," Bill said. "A sword you obviously need to start using."

What sword was Bill talking about? And how did Bill know that Trevor's "artifacts" weren't authentic?

☞ Turn to page 104 to find out!

Chapter 9

The Case of Phil the Warthog and Gideon's Spy

Mike Reed's new "Phil the Warthog: Warthog of War" comic was not just entertaining, but also a learning tool, or so he said. I only cared about the entertaining, but...

"I got the idea to use Phil to teach military history," said Mike. "So I decided to have Shady Tompkins let Phil in on a top secret government project: a time machine."

Mike held up a new edition of the comic. "In this issue he goes back to observe Gideon in the battle against the Midianites."

"Who's Gideon?" I asked. "And what's a medium light?"

"Gideon was a judge, Nick," said Bill. "About 3500 years ago he led the Israelites into battle against their oppressors, called the Midianites. Gideon's battle plans are still studied in military academies."

"You mean this is a Bible story?" I asked.

"Yeah, but I made a few changes," said Mike.

"Like inserting a mutant warthog from the 21st century?" asked Bill.

"Why don't you just read it? Let me know what you think," Mike replied.

The comic opened with Phil the Warthog emerging from what looked like a boulder. (There was an asterisk by the boulder that led to a footnote that read, "See Issue #12 in which Shady and Phil disguise the time machine as a boulder.")

As Phil – who was dressed in some sort of toga – left the boulder, he spied two men lurking behind a set of bushes. They were in similar dress. The men were whispering, but Phil couldn't understand them until he used the translator gadget Shady had given him.

"Here he comes along the trail," said one.

"You're right. It's Gideon, the guy who destroyed

our idol, Baal," said the other.

("Are those the Midianites?" I asked Bill. "No," said Bill, "I think they're Israelites who were worshiping a statue that Gideon destroyed.")

"Look out, Gideon!" Phil cried out.

Then there was a series of panels with Phil and Gideon fighting the two men, until the men ran from them.

"Thank you, my friend," said Gideon. "You are not from here, are you?"

"No, Gideon, I am from far away. But I have heard of you, and I believe in your battle against the Midianites and Amalekites, who have stolen your crops and livestock."

"How do I know, strange looking one, that you are not a spy for my enemy?" Gideon asked.

"I did save your life," said Phil.

"True," said Gideon. "I will trust you."

The next panels showed Gideon selecting the men who would go with him to battle. At first, 32,000 men came out to fight. (Mike didn't draw all 32,000 men, but it looked like a lot.)

But God told Gideon that he wanted fewer men to go out against the Midianites so the glory would go to

God, not Gideon's army.

So Gideon said, "If anyone is afraid, he can go home." And 22,000 men left.

But God said 10,000 was still too much.

So Gideon told the men to go down to the water to drink. Gideon observed which men put their heads down into the water, and which men used their hands

to scoop water to their mouths.

Those that scooped water to their mouths were the ones God told Gideon to choose. This ended up being only 300 men.

"That's not many," Phil said.

"This is what God wants," said Gideon. "But it is important that the Midianites don't learn how small our army is – it would ruin the battle plan."

That night as the 300 men prepared for battle, Gideon went to spy on the enemy. But while he was gone, Phil heard a ruckus on the edge of camp. He grabbed a spear and went to see what was wrong.

Two men were fighting. Phil told them to stop and asked them what was happening.

"My name is Jamin, and this man is a spy from the

Midianites. I stopped him before he could return to his camp to tell the enemy the size of our forces."

"He's lying," said the other man. "My name is Hirah, and he is the Midianite spy."

Phil had to figure out which was the real spy. He had an idea.

"Both of you," said Phil, "show me your provisions."

Both men had animal skin bags with provisions for the battle. Both men had the jars and trumpets that Gideon had instructed them to bring to the battle.

(I asked Bill why anyone would bring jars and trumpets to a fight, but he said it would be obvious later.)

Both had knives and bags of grain and dried fruit.

But Jamin also had a sling with five stones. Hirah had a sheep bladder full of water and a small cup.

Gideon returned to find the two men with Phil.

"I have good news," said Gideon, "I heard something in the Midianite camp that makes me sure we will win the battle."

"And I have captured a spy," said Phil, "It is..."

To Be Continued...

"So what do you think?" asked Mike.

"I'm not sure," said Bill. "I'm uncomfortable with the use of this fictional character in the Bible story. You did take liberties with the story."

"Like what?" I asked.

"Well, first of all, although Gideon did tear down the altar to Baal, he never got in a fight over it because Gideon's father, Joash, said if Baal was a real god, he could take care of himself."

"What else?" I asked.

"This whole bit about a spy in the Israelite camp is fictional. But my real problem is Phil the Warthog as a friend of Gideon's. You don't need to add fiction; the story of Gideon is fascinating enough on its own."

"What did you think, Nick?" Mike asked eagerly.

"It did get me interested in Gideon. I think I'll read his story. I wonder why the Bible is supposed to be about love, but it has so many battles. And which guy was the spy?"

"The spy was obvious," said Bill. "But your question before takes more thought."

So who was the spy? And why is there so much conflict in the Bible?

☞ Turn to page 106 to find out!

Chapter 10

The Case When Bill Goes to Peaces

I was really mad.

So mad that I almost didn't call Bill, because I knew he would be all calm and reasonable about everything.

I was sure the Kickies were responsible for trashing our Frisbees, and they needed to be held responsible for this insult to the Ultimates.

But you don't know what I'm talking about, do you? I'll fill you in.

Weather permitting, I spend every recess and lunch hour with friends playing Ultimate Frisbee. If

you've never played, it's a game that is kind of like soccer except instead of kicking the ball down the field, you pass a Frisbee.

We had a team, and we called ourselves the "Ultimates."

But on the same field at Elm Street Elementary, there are kids just as devoted to playing kickball. We call them the "Kickies."

Our school's playing field isn't huge, so sometimes our games collide. It's to be expected. But the Kickies make a big deal every time one of our players runs onto their part of the field.

And I can't count the times a great Ultimate play was ruined by the stupid kick ball coming onto our field.

So that's the background. Here's what had me furious.

All the playground equipment (jump ropes, basketballs, kick balls, Frisbees and such) is kept in the field shack. And this semester the field shack was under the rule of Paul Olive.

Paul checked out the equipment and checked it back in, and he was real picky.

You had to say, "Please," or he wouldn't hand you

a basketball.

You had to fill out the sign-up sheet just right (name, then your teacher, and then the time), or no jump rope.

So the other day at recess when I came to the shack to get the Frisbee, and Paul said no, I thought I had broken one of his rules.

"Okay, Paul, may I please check out a Frisbee?" I asked the second time.

"It's still no, Nick. Unless you want this." Paul held up the tattered remains of what looked like three Frisbees.

"What happened?"

"I can only guess," said Paul. "Someone must have broken in at night and destroyed them."

"Don't you lock the shed, Paul?"

"Of course I do, Nick. Do you think I don't know my job? I always use this." Paul held up the combination lock he used on the shed door latch.

"Who do you think did it?" I asked.

"Who do you think?" Paul responded knowingly.

I knew.

So I ran out to the field where the Kickies were playing. I went straight to the pitching mound where the Kickie I thought most likely responsible was standing, kick ball in hand: Chris Franklin.

"Why aren't you playing your stupid Frisbee game, Ten Toes?"

"Only my friends can call me that," I said.

"All right, I'll just call you 'doofus' then. But why aren't you playing your little girl game?"

"You know why, Chris. Because you broke into the equipment shed last night and destroyed the Frisbees. And you are going to pay the school to buy new ones."

"Yeah, right. Is your pig friend going to make me?"

"Bill isn't in this."

"Well, maybe he should be," said Chris. "I think it was one of your stupid Frisbee friends who wrecked your toys because he was tired of playing. And he wrecked the kick balls while he was at it."

"What are you talking about?" I said.

Chris rolled the kick ball toward the batter. It rolled erratically. It was obviously flat and had several punctures.

"I still say it was you," I said, "And you're going to pay."

"You want to fight about it?"

"Maybe," I replied.

"Maybe we could have a fight between the Kickies and the Ultimates," Chris said. "I know who has more practice kicking tail. Still, maybe you should call your pig friend."

So I did call Bill, and he agreed to meet me, Chris and Paul after school.

I introduced Paul to Bill. "So the stories are true," Paul muttered under his breath as he looked over Bill from head to hoof.

Bill ignored his stares and focused on examining the ruined Frisbees and punctured kick balls.

"If I'm not mistaken," said Bill, "and I rarely am, these Frisbees and this kick ball were damaged by dogs."

We examined the items more closely. There definitely were teeth marks on everything.

"You have a dog, don't you, Chris? A pit bull, isn't it?" I asked.

"You leave Mr. Happyface out of this!" said Chris. He'd named the dog when he was 3 years old.

"Is it possible you might have accidentally left the equipment shack open, Paul, and neighborhood dogs ruined the equipment?" Bill asked.

"No way," said Paul. "I could lose this job if I did

something like that. Someone must have gotten the combination to the lock.

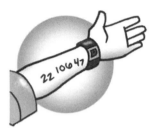

"In fact, look at the numbers on Chris's arm! That's the combination...on Chris's arm!"

There were numbers on Chris's forearm: 22, 106, 47.

"You're saying that's the combination to the lock, Paul?" Bill asked.

"It is," said Paul. "Chris must have broken into the shed and let his dog chew the equipment."

"I didn't do it," said Chris. "These numbers are just the answers to today's math quiz."

"I think I know all I need," said Bill. "Paul, do you know your words and actions almost led to a big fight?"

"What are you talking about?" said Paul.

"I'm saying you need to take responsibility for your actions. You did leave the door open last night, so I'm assuming the equipment was wrecked by neighborhood dogs.

"As for you, Nick, you need to try to be at peace with everyone, even Chris."

"Hey, Pig, I appreciate you being on my side," said

Chris. "But how did you know I was innocent?"

"'Innocent' isn't the word I'd choose. You could use the breastplate of righteousness, and you need to learn about the importance of peace as well."

How did Bill know Paul was responsible for the damaged equipment? And why is Bill talking about peace when he has been talking so much about weapons and war?

☞ Turn to page 108 to find out!

The Case of the Full Metal Trench Coat

Q: *How did Bill know so quickly that the trench coat wasn't real gold?*

A: Notice that Bill said "I feel" this is a fraud and that he didn't take it "lightly." Bill chose those words carefully.

Bill could feel, as Nick did, that the trench coat felt the same as it had before – it only looked different. If the trench coat really had been covered in gold it would have felt much heavier, and Bill probably would not have been able to toss it high in the air and catch it on his front legs.

Brewster had to admit his machine just temporarily colored clothes (silver, bronze or gold), and that he was going to take the money from the kids for himself.

It would be kind of cool to have clothes that could protect us from injuries, but Brewster had invented no such thing.

Q: *What was this other "armor" Bill was talking about?*

A: In the Bible, in the New Testament book of

Ephesians, chapter 6, Paul (who wrote the book as a letter) talks about putting on "the full armor of God." Although we don't have special clothes to keep us safe, God has some other ideas about how to protect us.

I'm sure Bill will have more to say about that protection. **READ ON!** ➡

The Case of the Warthog of War

Q: *What kind of weather would Phil have been looking for?*

A: When Bill read about Phil preparing for war against an invisible enemy, he had no doubt about the kind of weather the comic book warthog would want.

In sunny weather, it might be possible for invisible creatures to cast a shadow, but that was unlikely. But in rain, there surely would be an outline of where the rain hit the creatures, and there might be the added bonus of footprints in mud.

Q: *What did Bill mean when he talked about believing in invisible enemies?*

A: In Ephesians 6 (the same passage that talks  about the full armor of God), Paul writes about "spiritual forces of evil in the heavenly realms" – the forces of the devil.

A lot of people these days don't believe in the devil, but some of the toughest things we have to deal with in life are not what we see. Instead, they're things like the temptation to do wrong. We need help to deal with the forces of darkness that tempt us to do wrong.

That help comes from God. And from His armor. You'll read more about that armor in the next few chapters.

The Case of the Milk and Money Belt

Q: *How did Chris cheat in the first contest?*

A: Nick had told Bill that Chris was not trustworthy, so Bill was watching for Chris to try something tricky with the contest. And he did.

Bill noticed that Chris and Dwayne had a code set up.

For the whole milk, Dwayne said Chris would "totally" guess.

Then Dwayne said "nothing" could stop Chris when he got the non-fat. When Nick brought the two-percent, Dwayne said Chris would get that one "too." Bill figured Chris and Dwayne had set up code words in advance.

This proved true when Chris could not win a fair taste contest.

Q: *What was this "belt of truth" that Bill was talking about?*

A: In Ephesians 6, when Paul talks about the full armor of God, the belt is the first thing mentioned. A  belt was used in the same way then as it is now. We use a belt to keep our pants up; they used belts to hold clothes in place.

The truth works like that in life. When we lie, it's hard to hold things together, and we usually get caught (just like Chris was caught in his dishonesty).

But when we're honest and tell the truth, it's easier to hold things together, because people know they can trust us. We are safer telling the truth.

The Case of the Celebrity Shoes

Q: *Why did Bill think Cameron was dishonest?*

A: The letter was all the evidence Bill needed to know that Cameron wasn't telling the truth about the shoes. Bill knew the equipment manager of a British team did not write the letter.

First of all, the letter referred to the shoes as "tennis shoes." That is a common name for athletic footwear in America, but in England they are known as "trainers" or "runners."

The other piece of evidence was the word "soccer." In most of the world, including England, "football" is used for the game we call "soccer." (And our "football" is called "American football" elsewhere.) In fact, Manchester United players refer to their playing shoes as "football boots"!

Cameron had purchased cheap tennis shoes at a thrift store and kept the rest of the uniform money. He returned the money, and Blake's mother purchased yellow uniforms for the Lemon Streeters.

Q: *What are the Good News shoes?*

A: The Good News shoes that Bill referred to are

also from Paul's armor in Ephesians 6. Verse 6:15 talks about fitting feet with the "gospel of peace." "Gospel" means "good news."

Paul is teaching us to take the Good News of God's love everywhere we go, because all people need to know the Good News that God loves them.

The Case of the Flying Rocks

Q: *What did Bill see that proved Chris's guilt?*

A: Nick mentioned that Brandon had a well-stocked tool shed, and as Nick knew from playing Handyman Harry, that would include a variety of screwdrivers (at least two: a Phillips and a straight edge).

But Chris picked up a specific screwdriver and then seemed confident that he had ruined Bill's case. How would he know which screwdriver was used to sabotage Brandon's lawn mower unless he had done it himself?

Mr. Smith saw this, so Chris agreed that he would pay off the window repair by working at Mr. Smith's house (but Brandon continued to mow his lawn).

Q: *What is the other shield Bill was talking about?*

A: In Ephesians 6, Paul wrote about "the shield of faith." People today have a lot of strange ideas about faith. Some people say it doesn't matter what you believe in, as long as you have faith.

But the Bible makes it clear it's important that you have faith in God. Faith means you do what the Bible says, believing God will keep you safe. And that is the most important shield you can use!

The Case of the Edible Arrows

Q: *How could Bill prove Matt was lying?*

A: Bill had proof that Matt was lying about his eye when he answered the survey questions and said that he experienced the 3-D effects in the movie.

The way we see in three dimensions is through our eyes taking in things from different perspectives. Our brain combines those perspectives to help us see in 3-D.

If Matt was blind in one eye, he wouldn't have been able to see in 3-D. So he wouldn't have seen the lion "coming out of the screen."

Because Matt signed the survey card saying he saw the 3-D (a survey arranged by Bill, by the way), he ruined his chances for suing Charlie in court.

Q: *What are the enemy arrows Bill was talking about?*

A: Matt hadn't been hurt by a celery arrow. But he

was succumbing to another arrow. In the same

 passage that Paul wrote about the full armor of God in Ephesians 6, he also warned about "flaming arrows of the evil one."

These arrows are temptations, fears and doubts that keep us from having a good relationship with God. God wants to protect us from those arrows, but we have to seek His help.

He is more than willing to give it. All you have to do is ask!

The Case of the Hopeless Helmet

Q: *How did Bill observe that Zack didn't know about skateboard safety?*

A: Bill was, of course, already suspicious of Zack, but something that Zack did convinced Bill that Zack was not informed about equipment safety.

Zack put his whole right hand through the strap on his neck to scratch the stubble.

Bill knew that the helmet strap should be snug for safety. You should only be able to put two or three fingers through the strap when it is properly tightened – not your whole hand.

Zack agreed to shut down his business, mostly because of Bill's threat to call the police and the Better Business Bureau.

Q: *What is this "helmet of salvation" Bill was talking about?*

A: It's another part of the armor of God that Paul wrote about in Ephesians 6.

It's good to make sure you're physically safe when playing sports by wearing the right equipment. Even more important is being spiritually safe. The armor of God is meant to help keep us from doing wrong – from sinning. We all do wrong things – we all sin.

But we can ask God for forgiveness because Jesus died for us. That forgiveness is an important piece of equipment. We all need it to be truly safe!

The Case of the Pizza Sword

Q: *How did Bill know that Trevor's "artifacts" weren't authentic?*

A: The Bible in the museum provided the evidence that Trevor did not have Arthur's authentic artifacts.

Arthur, if he existed, lived in the 6th century AD according to Trevor. But that was about a thousand years before Gutenberg invented the printing press. Up until that time, books were copied by hand. But the Bible in the museum had printing that read "Family Tree."

If that wasn't proof enough, there was no English version of the Bible until after the time of Gutenberg.

Trevor admitted the items in his museum were fake, and agreed to return the sword to the pizza parlor and the money to those who paid to enter the museum.

Q: *What sword was Bill talking about?*

A: The sword Bill was referring to was the one Paul wrote about when he described the full armor of God in Ephesians 6: "the sword of the Spirit which is the Word of God." In other words: the Bible.

Bill told Trevor he needed to start using that other sword, the Bible.

If Trevor started reading and putting into practice the words of the Bible, he might be able to avoid the temptation to steal and lie. And he would learn about courage, honor and justice, the very things that make the stories of Arthur memorable to this day.

The Case of Phil the Warthog and Gideon's Spy

Q: *Who was the spy?*

A: Bill knew the captured spy part of the Gideon tale was fiction, but he knew which man was guilty within the story.

Hirah had a sheep's bladder full of water and a cup in his pack. The men God told Gideon to pick were those who cupped water from the stream with their hands. Hirah wouldn't have used his hands to get water if he had a cup. And if he hadn't used his hands, he wouldn't have been chosen to be among the 300 for the Israelite army.

Nick wanted to know what happened next in the story, but he didn't want to wait until Mike's next comic. So he went to read Judges 6 and 7 for himself.

Q: *Why is there so much conflict in the Bible?*

A: People who read the Old Testament today often are surprised at how much of it is about warfare. The

Bible is clear that when people live without God, there is bound to be hate and conflict.

But even if God doesn't call us to be warriors like Gideon, we can learn from his example. Gideon was a man who trusted God, and who allowed the glory of victory to go to Him.

The Case When Bill Goes to Peaces

Q: *How did Bill know Paul was responsible for the damaged equipment?*

A: Bill knew Paul wasn't telling the truth when he pointed to the numbers on Chris's arm and claimed they were the combination to the lock on the shed.

Bill explained that the numbers "22-106-47" do not make sense for a combination lock. Most combination locks have numbers from 0-40. No combination locks use three digit numbers.

So Chris was innocent of breaking into the shed (but not of cheating on the math quiz).

Paul was afraid of losing his equipment job for forgetting to lock the shed.

What really concerned Bill was that Nick and Chris seemed willing to fight over the broken Frisbees and balls. Bill didn't think it was worth fighting over.

Q: *Why is Bill talking about peace when he has been talking so much about weapons and war?*

A: Even though Scripture does talk about the reality of war and fighting in this world, and uses symbols  like the armor of God for fighting evil in the world, God wants us to seek peace.

Jesus said to pray for our enemies. If you have someone like Chris in your life, you should pray for him.

The real battle is to live for God, and to share His Good News with others.

The fun devotionals that help you grow closer to God.

Gotta Have God (for guys) and *God and Me!* (for girls) are packed with over 100 devotionals, plus memory verses, stories, journal space and fun activities to help you learn more about the Bible.

Gotta Have God for Guys 10-12, Vol. 1
ISBN 1-885358-98-9

Gotta Have God for Guys 10-12, Vol. 2
ISBN 1-58411-059-7

God and Me! for Girls 10-12, Vol. 1
ISBN 1-885358-54-7

God and Me! for Girls 10-12, Vol. 2
ISBN 1-58411-056-2

Journals just for you!

Want more ideas for quiet time with God? Get these devotional journals to help you know Him and understand the Bible better. Each book includes stories to make you think, plus plenty of space for writing prayer requests and praises.

My Prayer Journal
DB 46731
ISBN 1-885358-37-7

My Bible Journal
LP 46911
ISBN 1-885358-70-9

My Praise Journal
LP 46921
ISBN 1-885358-71-7

My Answer Journal
LP 46931
ISBN 1-885358-72-5

My Wisdom Journal
LP 46941
ISBN 1-885358-73-3